ALLAN DRUMMOND

CASEY JONES

FRANCES FOSTER BOOKS · FARRAR STRAUS GIROUX · NEW YORK

Library of Congress Cataloging-in-Publication Data
Drummond, Allan.
    Casey Jones / Allan Drummond. — 1st ed.
        p.   cm.
    "Frances Foster books"
    Summary: Illustrations and rhythmic text tell how the famous engineer, Casey Jones,
risks his own life to save others.
    ISBN 0-374-31175-7
    1. Jones, Casey, 1864–1900—Juvenile Fiction.   [1. Jones, Casey, 1864–1900—Fiction.
2. Railroads—Fiction.   3. Stories in rhyme.]   I. Title.
PZ8.3.D8445Cas   2000
[E]—dc21   99-22385

Listen!

—Want to hear the story of Casey Jones?

That's him!

Listen!

Wallace Saunders
engine wiper

Sim Webb
fireman

—Listen!

—Want to hear the story
from Wallace and Sim
of the railroad's greatest hero,
Casey Jones?
That's him!

John "Casey" Jones
engineer

Listen!

—Did you hear that whistle?
Listen!

Wooo . . . oooh!

It's Casey Jones.

Wooo . . . oooh!

The clock at the station
shows a minute to eight.
And they all say Casey Jones
has never been late.
It's Casey Jones.

Wooo . . . oooh!

Wooo . . . oooh!

With one hand on the whistle
and the other on the brake,
he's arriving on the Illinois 638.

Wooo . . . oooh!

In roars the engine
with a rush of steam,
and the stationmaster shouts,
"Where have you been?"

And all of a sudden
there's a mountain of smoke
and the platform's buzzing
with all kinds of folk.

The milk from the dairy
and mail from the town
are loaded on the brake car
as the people climb down.

Children at the windows,
and the telegraph boy
with a message from the company
in Illinois.

Wallace grabs the oil can,
and Sim swings the scoop,
and Casey at the whistle
gives a final toot.

Casey Jones! He's never been late,
hooting at the whistle of the 638.

Wooo . . . oooh!

Listen!

Now all of this happened
a hundred years ago,
but it's a story that everyone
ought to know,

'cause the railroad back then
was the mightiest thing,
and the loco engineer
was the Iron Horse King!

Casey Jones!
The Iron Horse King!

All across America,
the steel wheels rolled,
joining ocean to ocean
with the power of coal.

Long lines of wagons
taking people and freight
through the deserts
and the mountains,
linking state to state.

New opportunities

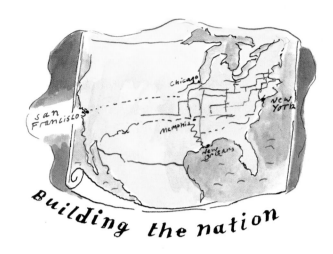

Building the nation

The railroads offered adventure to settlers as they spread out across the country...

...but their power brought destruction

the death of a way of life

disaster for the Native American

The freedom and the power
of the railroad track,
calling children and the grownups,
and they never looked back.

Wooo . . . oooh!

This train is bound for glory...

The music of the railroad

Goodbye and good luck!

The railroad became a mighty power as tracks all across America were joined together

Food for the city folk

Building the cities

Iron and steel works

Listen!

Now this is the story
of Casey Jones's fate
as he rolled into Memphis
on his 638.

He'd volunteered to drive
one stormy night
'cause another engineer
wasn't feeling right,

so with Sim as the fireman
they pulled through the yards
and an hour out of the city
started driving her hard.

The train was full of people
from all down the line—
mothers and children
all asleep at the time—

and the milk and the mailbags
from all over the state,
and everyone knew they were
running late.

Casey Jones,
he'd never been late,
hooting at the whistle of the 638!

Wooo . . . oooh!

In the deep of the night,
people turned in their beds,
hearing Casey's lonely whistle.
"There he goes!" they said.

But nobody told Casey
there was trouble ahead,
so he hung on with the throttle out,
and on they sped.

Now, a mile in the distance,
where no one could see,
was a bend in the track
by the Mississippi.

And two men were struggling
to clear the track
'cause a freight train had broken
and wouldn't move back.

So a flagman ran forward
with a red-and-white light,
which he swung at Sim and Casey
as they roared through the night.

But when Casey saw the signal
he was into the bend,
and the first thing he thought of
was the life of his friend.

"Jump, Sim, and save yourself!"
was the last thing Casey said
before his hands hit the levers,
trying to stop the train dead.

Casey could see that
they were rolling too fast,
and he figured that this journey
was going to be his last.

He slammed on the air brakes,
and pulled reverse gear,
then he hung on to the whistle pull
till all you could hear . . .

. . . was the screaming of the hooter . . .
the wail of the brakes . . .
and a terrible explosion
that made everything shake.

A cloud of smoke and ashes
and splinters of wood
rose up over the wreckage
where the freight train had stood.

Then there was silence . . .

. . . then a baby's cries.

And the flagman who came running
could not believe his eyes—

'cause from the brake car to the tender
the *whole* train was saved,
and one by one the passengers
stepped down in a daze.

"Where's Casey Jones?" Sim shouted
as he ran through the steam
to a pile of twisted wreckage
where the loco had been.

And as the dust settled
poor Casey lay dead.
Sim found him looking peaceful,
and somebody said,

"He's got one hand on the whistle
and the other on the brake
and his soul has gone to heaven
'board his 638."

Casey Jones! He'd never been late.
His soul went to heaven 'board a 638.

Now, all of this happened
a hundred years ago,
and it's a story that everyone
needs to know,

'cause the railroad back then
was the mightiest thing,
and the loco engineer
was the Iron Horse King.

Casey Jones! The Iron Horse King!

And out here in the backwoods
children still want to hear
the story of the railroad's
greatest engineer,

the man who gave his life
but who saved his train.
John Luther "Casey" Jones
was his name.

Listen!

Wooo . . . oooh!